MINI MEGA ACTIVITY BOOK

Have **FUN** completing this mini book
FILLED with ~1,000~ **MEGA** activities!

PUZZLE over **PIRATES**, DOODLE
on the **DINOS**, FIND the **FARM** animals,
and **EXPRESS** yourself with **EMOTIS**.

With over **500 STICKERS** to use
in the **BOOK** or wherever you want!

*make
believe
ideas*

TREASURE HUNT

FIND and **CIRCLE** the ITEMS below:

1 **FIVE** GOLD COINS

2 **FOUR** EARRINGS

3 **THREE** SWORDS

4 **TWO** JEWELS

5 **SIX** PARROTS

6 **COLOR** the TREASURE CHEST.

2

CARNIVORE COLORING

7 COLOR this picture of **TAMMY** the **T.REX**.

8 DRAW some SHARP **TEETH!**

9 DOODLE some more **PLANTS**.

EGG SEARCH

DRAW a **LINE** from each DINOSAUR
to its **MATCHING** colored **EGG**.

10

11

12

13

14 **DOODLE** some
SPOTS on SAMMY
the STEGOSAURUS.

EMOTI PATTERNS

Use **COLOR** to complete the **EMOTI** PATTERNS.

15

16

17

18

19

5

FARM FRIENDS

LOOK at the SCENE.
✓ the **BOXES**
when you **FIND** the
ANIMALS on the list.

20 **HOW MANY MICE** can you COUNT?

WRITE the ANSWER: ....

22	23	24	25	26
3 pigs	2 roosters	1 cow	2 horses	3 ducks

21 COLOR the TRACTOR.

27 5 chicks

28 4 sheep

29 2 turkeys

30 1 goat

31 1 fox

7

HOOK, LINE, AND SINKER

Can you find SIX DIFFERENCES between the SCENES?

✓ the boxes when you **FIND** them.

 32 1 33 2 34 3 35 4 36 5 37 6

DRAW THE LINE

38 **DRAW** a line from the START to FINISH. Visit all the EGGS, and don't go past any **VOLCANOES**.

Start →

39 **HOW MANY** VOLCANOES are there? WRITE the **ANSWER:** ....

Finish →

40 COLOR the **BONES**.

TASTY TREATS

CIRCLE the one that doesn't **MATCH** in each GROUP.

41

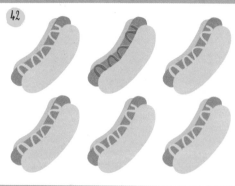

42

43

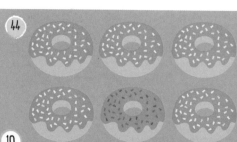

44

WORD FUN

45 COLOR the **ANIMALS.**

FIND the **WORDS** in the **WORD SEARCH.** **WORDS** can go **DOWN** or **ACROSS.**

a	r	b	n	o	s	w	h	l	p
s	n	r	t	q	r	x	o	z	w
o	b	a	r	n	t	r	r	a	e
k	r	n	a	y	r	b	s	n	u
a	i	e	c	l	w	o	e	u	p
s	y	o	t	l	k	d	f	h	i
h	j	m	o	s	u	t	d	j	g
e	a	u	r	t	r	a	u	n	s
e	i	p	i	z	b	a	c	w	y
p	s	h	c	h	i	c	k	c	l

46 barn

47 duck

48 chick

49 horse

50 pig

51 sheep

52 tractor

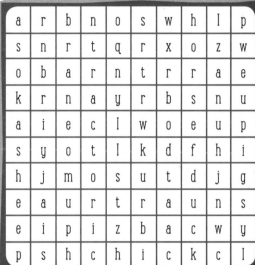

11

UP IN THE AIR

53 TRACE the CLOUDS.

54 CIRCLE three ORANGE **DRAGONFLIES.**

55 GUIDE the BUTTERFLY through the **MAZE** to reach its **FRIENDS.**

Start →

Finish ↓

12

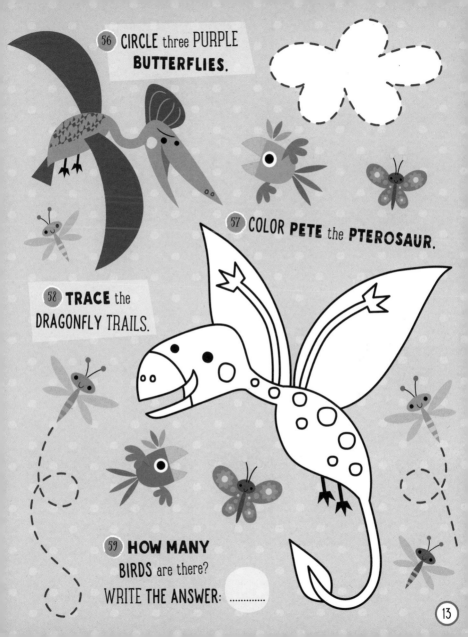

56 CIRCLE three PURPLE **BUTTERFLIES.**

57 COLOR **PETE** the **PTEROSAUR.**

58 **TRACE** the DRAGONFLY TRAILS.

59 **HOW MANY** BIRDS are there? WRITE THE ANSWER: ....

13

QUICK QUIZ

CIRCLE the PICTURES to answer the **QUESTIONS**.

60 **WHO** doesn't BELONG?

61 **WHAT** holds TREASURE?

62 **WHICH** of these would you find on a **BOAT**?

63 **WHAT** doesn't BELONG?

64 COLOR the **SHELLS**.

COUNTING CLAWS

Help **SAM** the **STEGOSAURUS** finish the SUMS.

65 $2 + 2 =$ ....

70 $5 + 4 =$ ....

66 $2 - 1 =$ ....

71 $4 - 1 =$ ....

67 $3 + 2 =$ ....

72 $3 + 4 =$ ....

68 $3 + 3 =$ ....

73 $4 + 4 =$ ....

69 $3 - 1 =$ ....

74 $5 + 5 =$ ....

TRICKY TRACKS

COLOR the **TRACTORS** to MATCH their TRAILERS.

75

76

77

78

79 Which **TRACTOR** is TOWING the **PIGS?** WRITE the COLOR:

SAILOR SPELLING

TRACE the **LETTERS** to help the **CAPTAIN** spell out the **WORDS**.

80  parrot

81 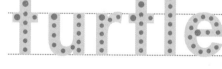 turtle

82 gem

83 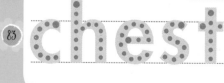 chest

84 **COLOR** the **TURTLE**.

SEARCH-O-SAURUS

FIND the **WORDS** in the **WORD SEARCH**. **WORDS** can go **DOWN** OR **ACROSS**.

h	q	w	e	h	r	c	t	o	p
s	p	i	k	e	s	a	a	c	x
p	x	s	x	v	o	r	e	x	e
i	h	o	p	r	i	n	x	w	x
f	o	o	t	p	r	i	n	t	t
s	r	x	c	x	a	v	o	r	i
c	n	s	l	v	p	o	k	e	n
a	q	l	a	t	t	r	x	r	c
l	x	p	w	b	o	e	l	a	t
e	r	l	s	a	r	x	s	r	x

85 carnivore

86 claws

87 extinct

88 footprint

89 horn

90 raptor

91 scale

92 spikes

93 **HOW MANY** BONES are there? **WRITE** the **ANSWER:** ....

18

PUTTING ON A SHOW

94 Can you **HELP** the **MUSICIAN** find his lost GUITAR?

Start

Finish

95 **COLOR** the audience **EMOTIS.**

FUN ON THE FARM

96 COPY the **HORSE**. Use the GRID to help you.

97 Now **COLOR** it in.

98 COPY the **COW**. Use the GRID to help you.

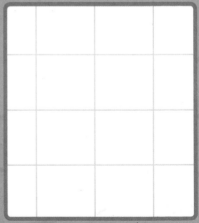

99 Now **COLOR** it in.

COLOR the LAMBS to **MATCH** their woolly SWEATERS.

21

WHAT'S IN A NAME?

Draw LINES to **MATCH UP** the dinosaur NAMES.

104 TRI

SAURUS

105 DIPLO

CERATOPS

106 STEGO

REX

107 T.

DOCUS

108 COLOR the DINOSAUR'S **SPOTS** BLUE.

COIN COUNT

Finish the **SUMS** to help the PIRATES count their **COINS**.

109

$1 + 4 = $ ....

114

$5 - 3 = $ ....

110

$4 - 1 = $ ....

115

$8 + 2 = $ ....

111

$5 + 1 = $ ....

116

$3 + 5 = $ ....

112

$2 + 5 = $ ....

117

$6 - 5 = $ ....

113

$5 - 1 = $ ....

118

$5 + 4 = $ ....

EMOTI-SHIRT

DRAW and **DOODLE** cool **EMOTI** designs on the T-SHIRTS.

119
120
121

DINO BUDDIES

Use the **CLUES** to find out which DINOSAUR is **ABI** the **ANKYLOSAURUS'** best **FRIEND**.

Sam the Stegosaurus

Dan the Diplodocus

Ann the Allosaurus

Sophie the Spinosaurus

Val the Velociraptor

Tom the T. rex

CLUE 1:
The dinosaur has green spots.

CLUE 2:
The dinosaur has orange spikes.

CLUE 3:
The dinosaur has big teeth.

125
CIRCLE Abi the Ankylosaurus's **FRIEND**.

126 **HOW MANY** EGGS are there? WRITE the **ANSWER**: ....

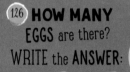

127 **COLOR** the dinosaur **FOOTPRINTS**.

26

LOTS OF DOTS

128 DRAW CLOUDS in the **SKY**.

129 **JOIN** the **DOTS** to **SEE** what's in the **FIELD**.

130 **HOW MANY RABBITS** are there? **WRITE** the **ANSWER**: ....

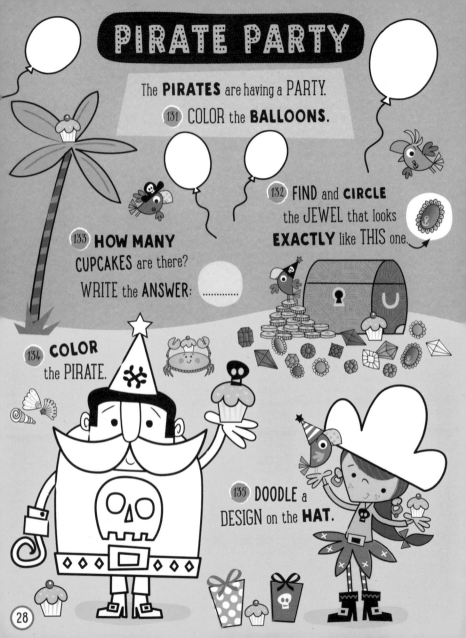

PIRATE PARTY

The **PIRATES** are having a PARTY.

131 COLOR the **BALLOONS**.

132 **FIND** and **CIRCLE** the JEWEL that looks **EXACTLY** like THIS one.

133 **HOW MANY** CUPCAKES are there? WRITE the **ANSWER**:

134 **COLOR** the PIRATE.

135 **DOODLE** a **DESIGN** on the **HAT**.

28

136 DRAW a MUSTACHE on the **PIRATE**.

137 DRAW an EYEPATCH on the **PIRATE**.

CIRCLE the ONE THAT'S DIFFERENT in each ROW.

138

139

140

COMPLETE the PIRATE SUMS.

141

$4 + 1 = $ ....

142

$6 - 3 = $ ....

143

$7 + 2 = $ ....

DINO FRIENDS

Can you find SIX **DIFFERENCES** between the SCENES?

✓ the boxes when you **FIND** them. 144 1 145 2 146 3 147 4 148 5 149 6

CRAZY CREATURES

DRAW funny FACES on the **ANIMALS**.

PICTURE PUZZLER

154 FIND and CIRCLE three **PURPLE** creatures.

WRITE the missing **LETTERS** to finish the WORDS.

155 e _ _

156 b _ n _

157 l _ a _

NAME GAME

DRAW a LINE to CONNECT the PIRATES to their NAMES.

159

158

Sailor Susan

Parrot Percy

160

161

First Mate Mike

162 **COLOR** the **PARROT**.

Captain Claude

PREHISTORIC PATTERNS

Use **COLOR** to complete the **PREHISTORIC** PATTERNS.

163

164

165

166

WONDERFUL WORDS

FIND the **WORDS** in the WORD SEARCH.
WORDS can go DOWN or **ACROSS**.

☑ each WORD when you've **FOUND** it.

a	s	n	a	p	p	l	r	s	a
p	t	t	r	s	h	e	e	p	s
p	r	f	a	r	l	a	m	f	r
l	a	z	c	h	i	c	k	e	n
e	w	n	o	y	r	c	l	f	a
b	b	c	w	o	r	z	l	a	n
c	e	t	r	y	m	b	n	r	f
b	r	c	o	k	l	a	u	m	s
g	r	p	d	u	c	k	b	e	r
k	y	t	r	a	i	l	e	r	m

167

apple ☐

168

chicken ☐

169

cow ☐

170

duck ☐

171

farmer ☐

172

sheep ☐

173

strawberry ☐

174

trailer ☐

35

SILLY SCRAMBLE

UNSCRAMBLE the WORDS below.
USE the PICTURES to **GUIDE** you.
Then **WRITE** the words on the DOTTED LINES.

EVCA

175 ....

DIRB

176 ....

ACONVOL

177 ....

ORWELF

178 ....

179 **HOW MANY**
DRAGONFLIES are there?
WRITE the **ANSWER:** ....

AVAST!

FIRST MATE MIKE is sorting the PIRATE PACKS.
CIRCLE the ONE that DOESN'T BELONG in each pack.

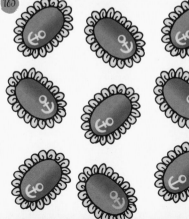

TERRIFIC TRACTOR

LABEL the **PICTURE** using the WORDS listed below:

- 184 tree
- 185 tire
- 186 sun
- 187 wheel
- 188 pig
- 189 light
- 190 trailer
- 191 farmer

f _ _ _ _ r

s _ _

t _ _ _

l i _ _ _ _

p _ _

tr _ _ l _ _

t _ _ _

w _ _ _ l

192 Now COLOR the TRACTOR.

EMOTI FUN

DESIGN your own **EMOTIS** for the things you think are really **FUN**.
Then write the **NAME** of the thing in the space beneath each **FRAME**.

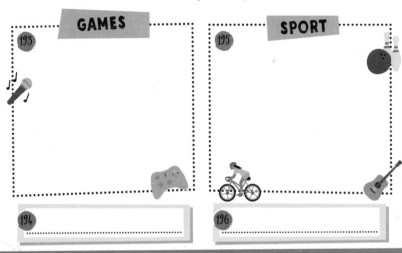

GAMES

193

SPORT

195

194

196

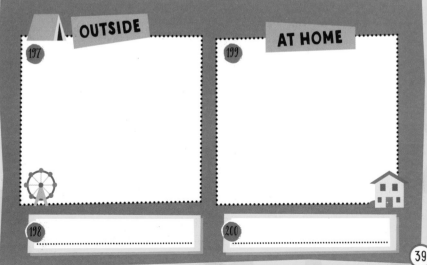

OUTSIDE

197

AT HOME

199

198

200

DIPLODOCUS MATH

Help **DAN** the **DIPLODOCUS** finish the SUMS.

201

$9 - 8 = \underline{}$

206

$6 + 1 = \underline{}$

202

$4 + \underline{} = 10$

207

$6 + \underline{} = 8$

203

$\underline{} + 4 = 5$

208

$\underline{} - 3 = 2$

204

$2 + \underline{} = 6$

209

$2 + \underline{} = 4$

205

$7 - 4 = \underline{}$

210

$6 + 3 = \underline{}$

RIGGING RACE

211 Draw a **LINE** from START to **FINISH**. Collect all of the **JEWELS** on the way, and **AVOID** the pesky PARROTS!

Finish

Start

212 HOW MANY JEWELS did you collect? WRITE the **ANSWER**: ....

213 COLOR the PARROTS.

HAPPY HARVEST

Use **COLOR** to complete the **HARVEST** PATTERNS.

214

215

216

217

42

X MARKS THE SPOT

FOLLOW the **LINES** to see who **REACHES** the **TREASURE.**

218

219

220

221 **COLOR** the **TREASURE.**

LABEL ME!

LABEL the **CREATURES** using the WORDS listed below:

| 222 claw | 223 leg | 224 scales | 225 spike | 226 teeth |
| 227 horn | 228 spots | 229 snout | 230 tail | 231 fin |

f _ _

s _ _ _ t

s _ _ l _ _

t _ _ _

s _ i _ _

t _ _ _ h

c _ _ w

h _ _ _ _

s p _ _ _ _

l _ _

44

RUSH HOUR

WRITE the ANSWER to the QUESTIONS below.

232 **HOW MANY** BUSES are there?

233 **HOW MANY** YELLOW CARS are there?

234 **HOW MANY** TRAIN CARS are there?

....

....

....

BACK ON TRACK

Draw LINES to match the ANIMALS to their FOOTPRINTS.

235

236

237

238

COLOR BY NUMBERS

239 Use the **KEY** below to **COLOR** the PICTURE.

47

SAVVY SPELLER

TRACE the **LETTERS** to help
SAILOR SERENA spell out the **WORDS**.

240 hat

241 coins

242 ship

243 flag

244 COLOR the **FLAG**.

48

BY THE BARN

Can you find FIVE **DIFFERENCES** between the SCENES?

✓ the **BOXES** as you **FIND** them.

 1 2 3 4 5

49

TIME FOR TEA

The **DINOSAURS** are HUNGRY.

250 FIND and CIRCLE **FIVE** pieces of **FOOD**.

251 Doodle **PATTERNS** on the **EGGS,** and then COLOR them in.

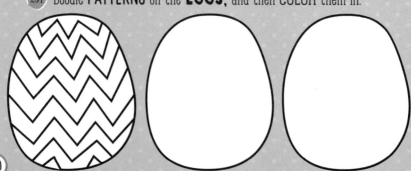

PIRATE COPY AND COLOR

Use the **GRID** to **FINISH** the ITEMS **BELOW**.

JOLLY ROGER

252

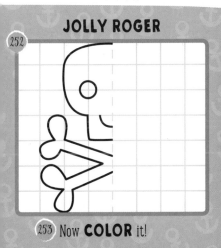

253 Now **COLOR** it!

SWORD

254

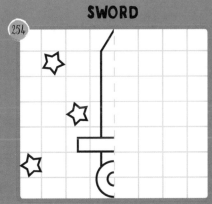

255 **DOODLE** some GEMS on the **HILT**.

TREASURE CHEST

256

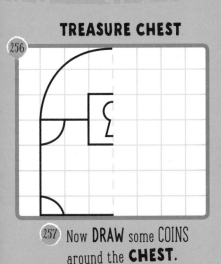

257 Now **DRAW** some COINS around the **CHEST**.

PIRATE

258

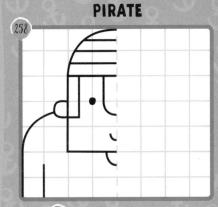

259 **DOODLE** a funny MUSTACHE and **BEARD**.

HEDGE MAZE

260 Follow the **TRAILS** to see who reaches the **MIDDLE** of the HEDGE MAZE.

Start

Start

turkey

goat

Finish

dog

Start

261 COLOR the **DOG**.

Write the **ANIMAL** that reached the MIDDLE of the MAZE.

262

FLORA'S FOOD

263 COLOR the **FOOD** on the **SHELVES**.

Look at the **SHELVES**. ✔ the **BOXES** when you **FIND** the things on the **LIST**.

264 3 apples

265 2 loaves of bread

266 4 carrots

267 1 piece of cheese

WHO'S WHO?

Look at the **PICTURES** BELOW.
WRITE the **NAMES** to **ANSWER** the QUESTIONS.

Who has **BLUE** SPOTS?

268 **E** ....

Bob

Charlie

Who has **RED** WINGS?

269 **C** ....

Rose

Mary

Who has a **PURPLE** TAIL?

270 **C** ....

Ellie

Chris

Who has **WHITE** TEETH?

271 **R** ....

Connie

Ryan

JOKING AROUND

Draw LINES to match the **ANSWERS** to the JOKES.

272 Why couldn't the PIRATE learn the **ALPHABET?**

It was on **SAIL!**

273 What SHIVERS at the bottom of the **OCEAN?**

He spent too **LONG** at **C!**

274 Why was the PIRATE SHIP so **CHEAP?**

Because they **ARRRRRRE!**

275 Why are **PIRATES** called PIRATES?

A NERVOUS **WRECK!**

FLOWER FUN

CIRCLE the **FLOWER** that doesn't BELONG in each **ROW**.

276

277

278

279 COLOR the **FLOWERS**.

280 DECORATE the **PETALS** with **PRETTY PATTERNS**.

DINO DISORDER

UNSCRAMBLE the WORDS below.
USE the PICTURES to **GUIDE** you.
Then **WRITE** the words on the DOTTED LINES.

NOEB

281 ....

HNSOR

282 ....

ETETH

283 ....

LAIT

284 ....

285 **HOW MANY**
FOOTPRINTS are there?
WRITE the **ANSWER:** ....

WORD SEARCH

286 COLOR the **PICTURES.**

Search the **GRID** for the **PIRATE** words below. **WORDS** can go DOWN or **ACROSS.**

✓ each WORD when you've **FOUND** IT.

a	c	d	s	w	o	r	d	f	p
f	g	s	t	i	j	c	l	t	i
l	u	v	l	w	m	a	p	t	r
a	r	a	y	z	r	i	a	p	a
g	t	r	e	a	s	u	r	e	t
v	y	i	x	r	a	o	c	m	e
t	s	h	i	p	y	q	k	t	y
u	i	j	k	f	e	y	t	n	d
p	a	r	o	l	z	v	w	u	b
h	y	m	e	r	m	a	i	d	o

287

flag

288

map

289

mermaid

290

pirate

291

ship

292

sword

293

treasure

58

PERFECT PORTRAITS

294 TRACE the **FARMER**.

295 DOODLE some **FLOWERS**.

296 COLOR the CORN.

297 DRAW **CARROTS** for the RABBIT.

298 DESIGN a **PATTERN** on the EGG.

UNDER THE SEA

299 DRAW some **WIGGLY LEGS** for the **JELLYFISH!**

300 CONNECT the **DOTS** to finish the **PICTURE.**

301 Now **COLOR** it in.

302 **HOW MANY** FISH are there? WRITE the **ANSWER:** ....

RAINY DAY

303 DRAW **RAINDROPS** in the SKY.

304 DOODLE some beautiful FLOWERS.

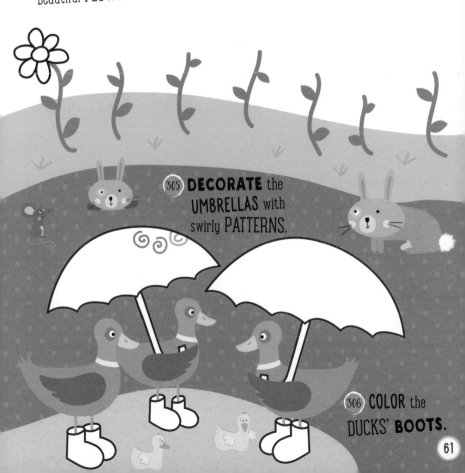

305 **DECORATE** the UMBRELLAS with swirly PATTERNS.

306 COLOR the DUCKS' **BOOTS**.

MY EMOTI DEN

DESIGN **EMOTI SIGNS** to put in your DEN.

307

KEEP OUT!

308

SHHH!

309

SECRET MEETING

310

COME IN

311 COLOR the **FUN** ACTIVITIES.

313 COLOR the tasty **SNACKS**.

312 Now CIRCLE your **FAVORITE**.

314 Now CIRCLE your top three SNACKS.

315 DOODLE **EMOTIS** on the BACKPACK

63

FOREST FUN

316 Finish **COLORING** the scene.

LOOK at the SCENE.
✓ the **BOXES** when
you **FIND** the
THINGS on the list.

317

1 T.rex ☐

318

2 birds ☐

319

3 eggs ☐

320

1 pink butterfly ☐

321 3 bones

322 4 purple flowers

323 1 dragonfly

324 2 velociraptor

KEEP FIT

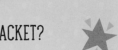

325 Can you **HELP** the **ATHLETE** find her TENNIS RACKET?

Start

Finish

326 **COLOR** the sporty **EMOTIS**.

BIRDS OF A FEATHER

327

FIND and CIRCLE the **PARROTS** that look EXACTLY like these.

328

329 **COPY** the **ANCHOR**. Use the GRID to help you.

330 Now **COLOR** it in.

FIND THE DIFFERENCE

Can you find **FIVE DIFFERENCES** between the SCENES?

✔ the boxes when you **FIND** them.

 1　 2　 3　 4　 5

JURASSIC JUMBLE

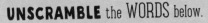

UNSCRAMBLE the WORDS below.
USE the PICTURES to **GUIDE** you.
Then **WRITE** the words on the DOTTED LINES.

336 **D N S A U R I O**
....

337 **W L C A**
....

338 **B N E O**
....

339 **E L A F**
....

340 **E V C A**
....

341 **G E G**
....

342 **W N G I**
....

343 **V L O A C O N**
....

344

FIND the WORDS in the WORD SEARCH. WORDS can go DOWN or **ACROSS.**

b	o	c	a	v	e	l	o
c	a	l	z	e	g	g	i
d	l	e	a	f	n	o	v
i	d	i	n	s	r	a	o
n	w	l	j	c	a	w	l
o	i	v	o	l	y	n	c
s	n	a	e	a	i	o	a
a	g	u	w	w	i	n	n
u	d	r	n	c	l	a	o
r	m	w	b	o	n	e	i

MORNING ALARM

345 COLOR the **ROOSTER**.

346 COLOR the **ALARM CLOCK**.

347 DRAW the HANDS on to show **SEVEN** o'clock.

348 **HOW MANY** CHICKS are there? WRITE the **ANSWER**: ....

PLENTY OF FISH

Follow the **LINES** to see which **PIRATE** has caught the **FISH**.

349

350

351

352 **COLOR** the **RAFT**.

353 **HOW MANY** **PARROTS** are there? **WRITE** the **ANSWER:**

DISCOVERY DINO

FIND and CIRCLE the missing FIVE DINOS:

354 355 356 357 358

TREASURE ISLAND

The **PIRATES** have found an **ISLAND** of TREASURE!

360 **COLOR** the PIRATE'S HAT.

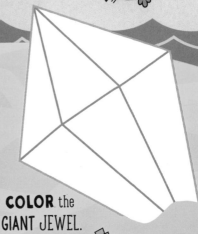

361 **COLOR** the GIANT JEWEL.

362 TRACE the **TRAILS** and FIND the **CRAB'S** JEWELS.

363 CIRCLE the **MERMAID** NECKLACE.

364 **HOW MANY** BLUE JEWELS can you **COUNT?**

365 **COLOR** the **PIRATE.** Use the **COLORED DOTS** to **GUIDE** you.

366 **COLOR** the **BARREL** of **JEWELS.**

75

PARTY TIME

HELP **FARMER** FRED prepare for a **PARTY**.

367 DRAW party **HATS** on the SHEEP.

368 Use **COLOR** to FINISH the CAKE.

369 **HOW MANY** CANDLES are there? WRITE THE ANSWER: ....

CONNECT AND COPY

DRAW A LINE from each **BONE** to the
MATCHING colored **DINOSAUR**.

370 371 372

373 COPY the **PICTURE.**
Use the GRID to **HELP** you.

374 THEN **COLOR** it in!

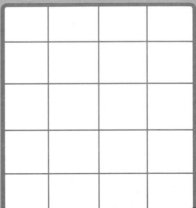

ANIMAL ROWS

CIRCLE the **ONE** that **DOESN'T** belong in each **ROW**.

SILLY SCENE

This **SCENE** isn't quite **RIGHT!**
FIND **SIX** THINGS that **DON'T BELONG.**

✔ the **BOXES** when you **FIND** them.

380   381   382   383   384   385

PIRATE PUZZLE

UNSCRAMBLE the WORDS below.
USE the **PICTURES** as a GUIDE.

EJLWE

386 ....

ARPORT

387 ....

TAEIRP

388 ....

HTSEC

389 ....

390 **HOW MANY** SHELLS
can you **COUNT?**
WRITE the **ANSWER:** ....

80

CANNONBALL COUNT

Finish the **SUMS** to help the CAPTAIN count the **CANNONBALLS**.

391 $6 + \text{......} = 10$

396 $11 - 2 = \text{......}$

392 $2 + 4 = \text{......}$

397 $8 - \text{......} = 2$

393 $7 + \text{......} = 9$

398 $7 - 3 = \text{......}$

394 $4 + 4 = \text{......}$

399 $10 - \text{......} = 5$

395 $8 + \text{......} = 10$

400 $9 - 6 = \text{......}$

GOING DOTTY

401 **CONNECT** the DOTS to **FINISH** the PICTURE.

402 THEN **COLOR** it in!

403 **HOW MANY** FISH are there? WRITE the **ANSWER**: ....

404 **COPY** the COLORS of the BIG underwater **VOLCANO** to FINISH the SMALLER one.

82

MYSTERY EGG

405 **FOLLOW** the LINES to see **WHICH HEN** laid the **COLORFUL** EGG.

406 **HOW MANY** WHITE EGGS can you **SEE?**
WRITE the ANSWER: ....

407 **COLOR** the HENS to FINISH the SCENE.

ANCHORS AWAY!

408 FOLLOW the **ROPES** to see which BOAT has DROPPED its **ANCHOR**.

409 DOODLE a **PIRATE** DESIGN on the SAIL.

410 **HOW MANY** FISH can you COUNT? WRITE the **ANSWER:** ....

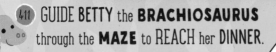

DINNER DASH

411 GUIDE BETTY the **BRACHIOSAURUS** through the **MAZE** to REACH her DINNER.

412 **COLOR** TERRY the PTERODACTYL.

Start

Finish

413 **HOW MANY** EGGS can you COUNT? ....

85

BOTTOM OF THE SEA

414 COLOR the **SHIPWRECK.**

415 HOW MANY SEASHELLS can you COUNT?

....

416 GUIDE the **FISH** through the MAZE to REACH his FRIENDS. **WATCH OUT** for the SEAWEED!

Start →

Finish ↓

417 **COLOR** the OCTOPUS.

418 Circle FIVE **YELLOW** fish.

14
15
13 16
19 20
10 17
11 18
12 21 22 1
9 2
8 3
5 4
7 6

419 **JOIN** the **DOTS** to REVEAL who's **LURKING** in the DEEP.

420 Then **COLOR** it in.

BUSY FARM

421 HOW MANY TRACTORS can you **COUNT?** ....

422 HOW MANY MICE can you **COUNT?** ....

423 HOW MANY SHEEP can you **COUNT?** ....

424 HOW MANY DUCKLINGS can you **COUNT?** ....

TRACE AND SEE

425 **COLOR** the FLOWERS.

426 **TRACE** the LINES to see WHO'S in the CAVE.

427 Then **DRAW** a FACE.

428 Now add COLOR!

MY FRIENDS

In the FRAMES, **DRAW** your FRIENDS as **EMOTIS**.
Then WRITE their **NAME** underneath!

429

430

431

432

433

435

434

436

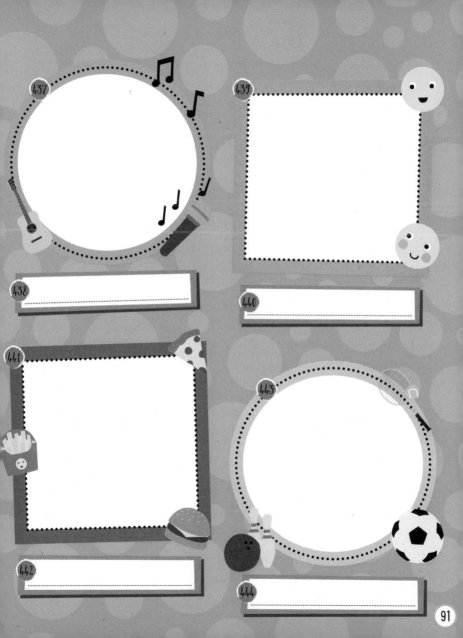

437

438

439

440

441

442

443

444

CAPTAIN'S KITCHEN

445 COLOR

CAPTAIN CALLUM'S KITCHEN.

446 DECORATE the CUPCAKES with YUMMY TOPPINGS.

FIND the THING that **DOESN'T** BELONG on **EACH** SHELF.

447

STARRRVING
YO, HO, DOUGH!
STARTERS OF THE SEVEN SEAS
CAPTAIN'S COOKBOOK
STEWS FOR CREWS
BAKING FOR PIRATES

448

P   S

449

450 **DOODLE** a **YUMMY** plate of **FOOD** for the **PIRATES.**

451 **THEN COLOR** it in.

452 **HOW MANY** VEGETABLES can you COUNT? **WRITE** the **ANSWER:** ....

EMOTI PAIRS

DRAW LINES to MATCH the PAIRS.

453   454   455   456   457   458

TRACE AND SEE

FIND the **MISSING LETTERS** to help **ADAM** the **ALLOSAURUS** **SPELL** out the **WORDS.**

459 **COLOR** ADAM the **ALLOSAURUS.**

460 c l _ w

461 b _ n e s

462 t a _ l

463 _ e e t h

464 **COLOR** the **BONES.**

465 **FIND** and **CIRCLE** **FIVE DRAGONFLIES.**

466 **HOW MANY** **BONES** are there? WRITE the **ANSWER:** ....

WHIRRING WINDMILL

It's **SPRING TIME** in the **WINDMILL** FIELD.

467 **COLOR** the **WINDMILL**.

468 **HOW MANY** SHEEP can you COUNT? WRITE the **ANSWER**:

....

469 **DRAW** more SEEDS to **FEED** the CHICKS.

470 **CIRCLE SEVEN** **FLOWERS**.

471 DRAW more **APPLES** on the TREES.

472 **DECORATE** the TRACTOR.

473 **DRAW** a DRIVER.

97

CARLA'S COLLECTION

FINISH the **SUMS** to HELP **CAPTAIN CARLA** count the JEWELS.

 474    9   + ...   =   11

475    4   +   9   =    ....

476   12   −   ....   =    6

 477    ....   +   7   =   14

VOLCANO VIEW

478 COLOR the SCENE to FINISH the **VOLCANO** VIEW.

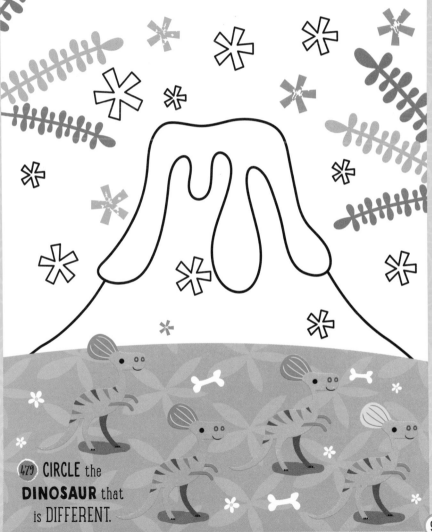

479 CIRCLE the **DINOSAUR** that is DIFFERENT.

SUPER STAMPS

Use **COLOR** and DOODLES to **CREATE** your own **STAMPS**.
YOU could **DRAW** your **FRIENDS**, ANIMALS, or **FAVORITE** PLACES.

480

481

482

483

484

485

DINO ART

486 **CONNECT** the **NUMBERED DOTS** to **COMPLETE** the **PICTURE.**

487 Then **COLOR** it in!

488 **COLOR** the **LAVA.**

489 **FIND** and **CIRCLE** the **ANT.**

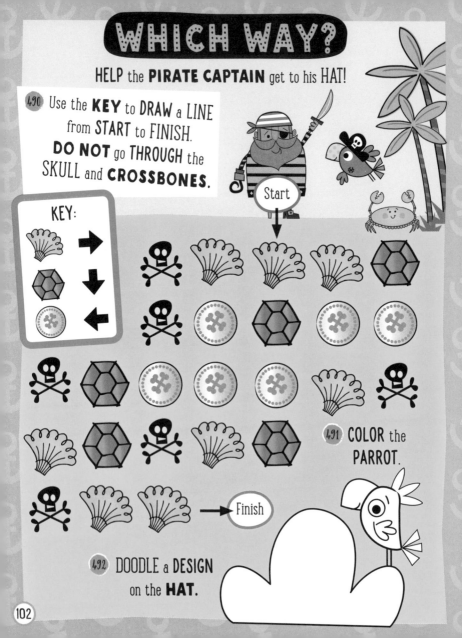

WHICH WAY?

HELP the **PIRATE CAPTAIN** get to his HAT!

490 Use the **KEY** to DRAW a LINE from **START** to FINISH. **DO NOT** go THROUGH the SKULL and **CROSSBONES**.

Start

KEY:

Finish

491 COLOR the PARROT.

492 DOODLE a DESIGN on the **HAT**.

102

TREASURE SEEKERS

Who has **FOUND** the **MOST JEWELS**?
COUNT the **JEWELS** for each **FRIEND**, and **WRITE** the **TOTAL** BELOW.

493

494

495

496 CIRCLE SEVEN **GOLD COINS.**

T.REX TROUBLE

LOOK at the **PICTURES.** WRITE the **LETTER** to answer the QUESTIONS below.

A

B

C

D

E

F

G

H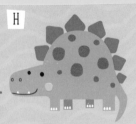

I

497 Who has **PURPLE SPIKES?**

....

498 Who has a **CURLY TAIL?**

....

499 Who has **THREE HORNS?**

....

ANIMAL FUN

500 **COPY** the **CHICKEN.** Use the **GRID** to **HELP** you.

501 **DOODLE** some **APPLES** on the **TREE.**

502 **COLOR** the **FLOWERS.**

PICTURE PERFECT

503 TRACE the **LETTERS** to reveal what the **PARROT** is SAYING.

polly

504 HOW many **PALM TREES** can you COUNT? **WRITE** the ANSWER: ....

505 Use the **KEY** below to **COLOR** the PICTURE.

1 2 3 4 5 6 7 8

FUNNY FACES

DOODLE EMOTI FACES in the **YELLOW** CIRCLES.

506

507

508

509

510

511

512

513

DINO DOODLES

514 Copy **TINA** the **TRICERATOPS**. Use the **GRID** to **GUIDE** you.

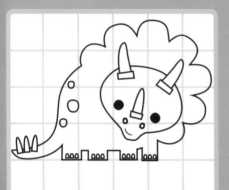

515 Then **COLOR** her in!

516 Use the **GRID** to finish the **DINO FOOTPRINT**.

517 Use the **GRID** to finish the **DINO EGG**.

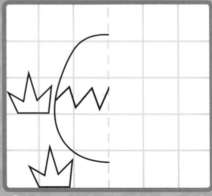

518 Doodle **COLORFUL SPOTS** on it!

PRIZE PUMPKINS

The **FARMERS** are competing to GROW the **BIGGEST PUMPKINS**.
519 **CIRCLE** the BIGGEST one.

520

521

DRAW FACES on
the **PUMPKINS.**

522 **523** **524**

525 **COLOR** the TROPHY.

WHO'S WHO?

Look at the **PICTURES** BELOW.
WRITE the NAMES to **ANSWER** the QUESTIONS.

Who has a **PINK** BANDANA?

526 **C** ....

Who has **ONE** GOLD EARRING?

527 **G** ....

Who has a **PARROT**?

528 **J** ....

Who is wearing **PURPLE** PANTS?

529 **S** ....

Who has a **HEART** TATTOO?

530 **R** ....

Who is PLAYING the **ACCORDION**?

531 **S** ....

Rodney

Padma

Claude

Steve

Jenny

Claire

Gregory

Susan

MOLTEN MATHS

HELP **TOM** the **T.REX** finish the SUMS.

532 $7 + 4 = \ldots$

533 $13 - 3 = \ldots$

534 $10 + \ldots = 15$

535 $\ldots + 2 = 8$

MY EMOTI DESIGNS

DESIGN new **EMOTIS** for these **DIFFERENT** things:

536

CAMPING

537 **DINOSAUR**

538

HOMEWORK

539 **COOKING**

540 CASTLE

541

SCHOOL

542

SURFING

543 A SELFIE

MOMMY MIX-UP

DRAW lines to MATCH the **BABY ANIMALS** to their MOMS.

544

545

546

547

114

PARROT PANIC

FIND all the **WORDS** in the **WORD SEARCH**.
WORDS can go **DOWN** or **ACROSS**.

548 anchor

549 cannon

550 flag

551 island

552 jewel

553 parrot

554 rigging

555 ship

556 skull

s	h	q	f	y	a	s	d	u	q
k	p	t	r	f	j	u	k	b	l
u	a	x	i	l	e	s	a	s	z
l	r	e	g	a	n	c	h	o	r
l	r	j	g	g	a	r	r	t	q
a	o	e	i	e	c	n	m	n	c
f	t	w	n	c	a	n	n	o	n
o	x	e	g	r	t	s	x	t	d
i	s	l	a	n	d	x	o	s	i
v	d	c	s	n	s	h	i	p	o

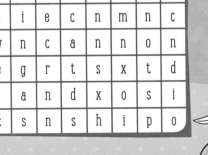

557 **COLOR** the **PARROTS**.

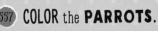

115

HOIST THE COLORS!

558 COLOR the **PIRATE** SHIP.

559 DECORATE the FLAGS.

560 DRAW a PIRATE in the **PORTHOLE**.

DINO DESIGNS

USE your COLORS to COMPLETE the DESIGNS.

561

562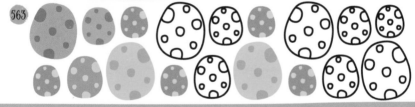

563

564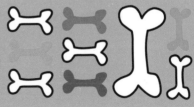

565

AHOY, ME HEARTIES!

566 **DOODLE** a cool **DESIGN** on the **BANDANA.**

567 **COLOR** the **PIRATES.**

568 Give them **NAMES:**

....

569 HOW many **BUCKETS** can you **SEE?**
WRITE the **ANSWER:** ....

HUNGRY PIGS

570 GUIDE the **PIG** through the MAZE to reach his DINNER.

571 TRACE a CURLY TAIL for **PERCY** the **PIG!**

Start

Finish

572 COLOR the YUMMY **APPLES.**

SUPER STARS

573 TRACE the **DOTS** to create **PATTERNS** in the NIGHT SKY.

574 Use COLOR to **COMPLETE** the SCENE.

575 DRAW another **SNAIL**.

576 **CIRCLE** the FLOWER that DOESN'T match.

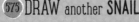

120

FAVORITE FLORA

DRAW a **LINE** from each **PTEROSAUR**
to the matching **COLORED** FLOWER.

577  green

578  blue

579 purple

580  red

WORDS AHOY!

UNSCRAMBLE the WORDS below.
USE the **PICTURES** as a GUIDE.

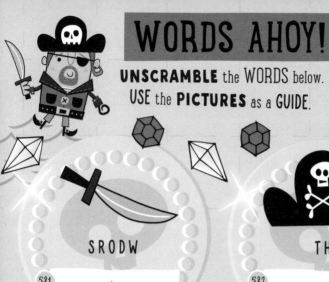

SRODW

581 ....

THA

582 ....

AMP

583 ....

OINCS

584 ....

585 **HOW MANY** RED RUBIES
can you **COUNT?**
WRITE the **ANSWER:** ....

122

ODD ONE OUT

CIRCLE the one that **DOESN'T** belong in each **GROUP**.

586

587

588

589

PARROT GRUB

Look at the **PICTURES** BELOW.
WRITE the **NAMES** to **ANSWER** the QUESTIONS.

Who has a **GREEN** BEAK?

590 **P** ....

Who has **ORANGE** WINGS?

591 **H** ....

Who has an **ANCHOR** TATTOO?

592 **M** ....

Who is wearing a
BLUE BANDANA?

593 **F** ....

Who has a **YELLOW** tail?

594 **D** ....

Pia

Fiona

Harry

Dave

Clive

Percy

Darcy

Mike

595 **COLOR** the CUPCAKES.

124

SKY SCENE

596 CONNECT the **DOTS** to reveal the PICTURE.

597 THEN **COLOR** it in!

598 How many **DRAGONFLIES** can you **COUNT?**

599 How many **BIRDS** can you **COUNT?**

600 How many **FLOWERS** can you **COUNT?**

601 How many **CLOUDS** can you **COUNT?**

SHARK ALERT

602 COLOR the PIRATE ship.

603 GUIDE the PIRATE SHIP through the MAZE to reach the TREASURE. WATCH OUT for SHARKS!

Start

Finish

604 COLOR the SHELLS.

HIDE AND SEEK

FIND and CIRCLE the **DINOSAURS** that look EXACTLY like THESE four:

605   606   607   608

FARMYARD FRIENDS

COPY the **PICTURES**. Use the **GRIDS** to **HELP** you.

609
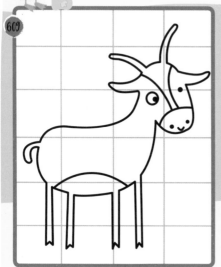
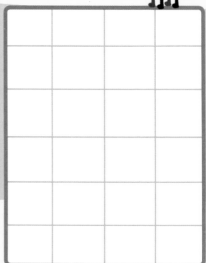

610
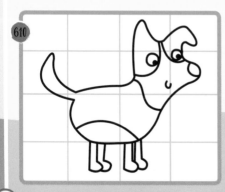

611

612

613 NOW COLOR them in!

DESERT ISLAND

Find all **EIGHT EMOTIS WORDS** in the **GRID**.
WORDS can go **DOWN** or **ACROSS**.

614 camera

615 fish

616 flamingo

617 flip-flops

618 magazine

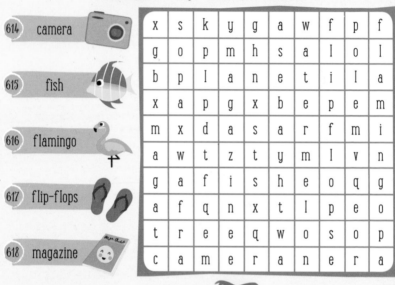

x	s	k	y	g	a	w	f	p	f
g	o	p	m	h	s	a	l	o	l
b	p	l	a	n	e	t	i	l	a
x	a	p	g	x	b	e	p	e	m
m	x	d	a	s	a	r	f	m	i
a	w	t	z	t	y	m	l	v	n
g	a	f	i	s	h	e	o	q	g
a	f	q	n	x	t	l	p	e	o
t	r	e	e	q	w	o	s	o	p
c	a	m	e	r	a	n	e	r	a

619 plane

620 tree

621 watermelon

622 **DRAW EMOTIS** of the **THREE THINGS** you'd **TAKE** to a **DESERT ISLAND!**

WHICH WORD?

DRAW lines to FINISH each PIRATE phrase.

623 X MARKS THE . . .

624 WALK THE . . .

625 SHIVER ME . . .

PLANK!

TIMBERS!

SPOT!

626 **COLOR** the JEWELS.

SUPER SCENE

Can you find SIX DIFFERENCES between the SCENES?

✓ the BOXES when you FIND them. 627 1 628 2 629 3 630 4 631 5 632 6

132

SHIPWRECKED!

The **SHIPWRECKED PIRATES** are HUNGRY!
Find and circle **SIX** pieces of FOOD.

✓ the boxes when
you **FIND** them.

633 1 634 2 635 3

636 4 637 5 638 6

639 **DOODLE** PATTERNS on the SHELLS.

133

STARGAZING

FINISH the SUMS to COUNT the STARS.

640  + = ...

645  + = ...

641 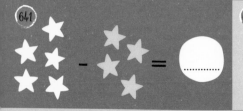 − = ...

646 − = ...

642 + = ...

647 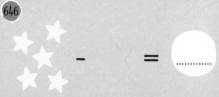 + = ...

643 + = ...

648 + = ...

644 − = ...

649 − = ...

CAPTAIN'S HAT

650 CONNECT the **DOTS** to finish the **PIRATE**.

651 Now **COLOR** him in.

652 FIND and CIRCLE three **CRABS**.

FIERCE FRAMES

COLOR the PICTURES in the **FRAMES**.

654

653

655

656 DRAW funny **HATS** on the DINOSAURS.

657 COLOR **ORANGE** stripes on **DAVE** the **DIPLODOCUS**.

658 DRAW a COLORFUL **DINOSAUR EGG** in the **FRAME**.

STORMY NIGHT

✓ **LOOK** at the **SCENE.**
the **BOXES** when you
FIND the **ITEMS** on the list.

659
2 bottles ☐

663
3 balloons ☐

660
2 sharks ☐

664
3 pirates ☐

661
4 skulls ☐

665
4 shells ☐

662
1 parrot ☐

666
1 anchor ☐

667 **COLOR** the **RAINDROPS.**

FARMYARD ART

Use the **GRIDS** to FINISH the **PICTURES** below.

TRACTOR

668

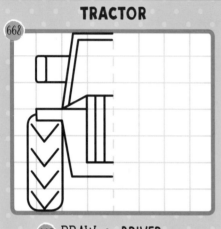

669 DRAW the **DRIVER**.

PIG

670

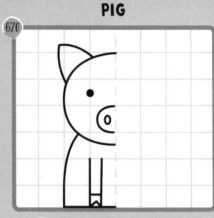

671 COLOR the pig PINK.

SCARECROW

672

673 DRAW a silly **FACE**.

CAT

674

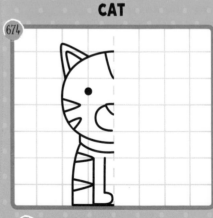

675 DRAW some curly **WHISKERS**.

DINO DRAWING

DOODLE **DETAILS** to create your own **DINOSAUR**.

676 **DRAW** more **SPIKES**.

677 **DRAW** some **SPOTS**.

678 **COLOR** the DINO a BRIGHT color.

BURIED TREASURE

COUNT the JEWELS to see which **PIRATE** has the most BURIED TREASURE.

679 WRITE the **ANSWER:** ....

680 WRITE the **ANSWER:** ....

681 COLOR the **TROPHY**.

TRACE RACE

TRACE the LETTERS to help the UNDERWATER **CREATURES** spell out the WORDS.

682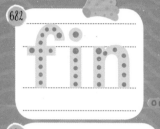
fin

683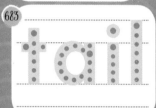
tail

684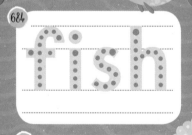
fish

685
shell

686 **HOW MANY** FISH can you COUNT?
WRITE the ANSWER: ....

ANIMAL OPPOSITES

DRAW **LINES** to match the OPPOSITES.

687
dry

awake

688
asleep

in front

689
big

wet

690
outside

inside

691
behind

small

CITY SCENE

Can you find FIVE **DIFFERENCES** between the SCENES?

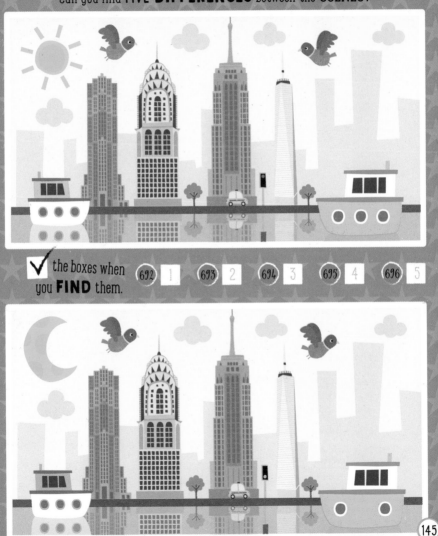

✓ the boxes when you **FIND** them.

692 | 1   693 | 2   694 | 3   695 | 4   696 | 5

DINO WORLD

✓ LOOK at the SCENE. ☑ the BOXES when you FIND the ITEMS on the list.

697
1 volcano ☐

701

3 dinosaurs ☐

698

2 birds ☐

702
2 eggs ☐

699
4 trees ☐

703

2 butterflies ☐

700

5 rocks ☐

704

4 bones ☐

146

705 Use COLOR to FINISH the SCENE.

SNACK TIME

707 **FINISH** COLORING the yummy TREATS.

708 **DRAW** your own EMOTI SNACKS here.

DINO DETAILS

CIRCLE the PICTURES to ANSWER the QUESTIONS.

709 **WHO** has the **LONGEST NECK?**

Pat

Dan

Bruno

710

WHICH of these can **HATCH?**

rocks

footprints

egg

711

WHICH one is **DIFFERENT?**

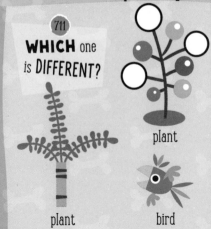

plant

plant

bird

712 **ADD** COLOR to the **PAGE.**

GOING TO MARKET

FINISH the sums and help **FARMER FLORA** COUNT what she **BOUGHT** at market.

713

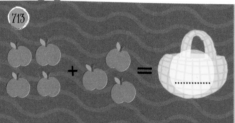 = ...

717

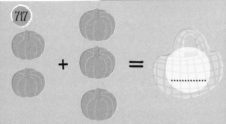 = ...

714

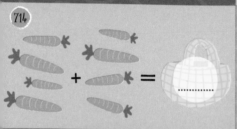 = ...

718

 = ...

715

 = ...

719

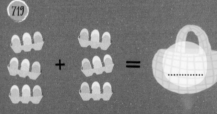 = ...

716

+ = ...

720

+ = ...

SAILOR SALLY'S MAZE

721 **GUIDE** SAILOR SALLY through the MAZE to REACH CAPTAIN CHRIS.

Start

Finish

722 **COLOR** the CAPTAIN.

723 **TRACE** the **LETTERS** to reveal the MESSAGE in the BOTTLE.

help

AT THE ZOO

This SCENE isn't RIGHT!
Circle **EIGHT** things that **DON'T BELONG.**

✔ the boxes when
you **FIND** them.

| 724 | 1 | 725 | 2 | 726 | 3 | 727 | 4 |
| 728 | 5 | 729 | 6 | 730 | 7 | 731 | 8 |

152

732 HOW MANY
PARROTS can you see?
WRITE the **ANSWER:** ....

HAPPY HORSES

733 Find and CIRCLE **FOUR** BROWN horses.

734 **COLOR** the CLOUDS.

LOOK at the PICTURES and **FINISH** the ANIMAL NAMES.

735 p _ _

736 _ o r _ e

WATER BABIES

DRAW a **LINE** from each BABY DINOSAUR
to its **MATCHING** colored **DADDY**.

737

green

738

blue

739

orange

740

purple

COUNTING CHICKENS

COUNT the pictures to help **FARMER TED**
count his **EGGS** and CHICKENS.

741 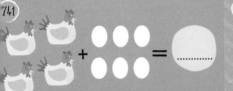 = ...

746 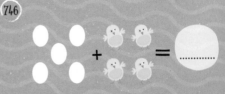 = ...

742 ⬭⬭⬭ ⬭⬭⬭ − 🐤🐤 = ...

747 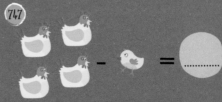 = ...

743 🐔 + 🐤🐤 🐤🐤 🐤🐤 = ...

748 🐤 🐤🐤 + ⬭⬭ = ...

744 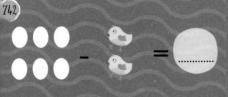 = ...

749 🐔🐔 🐔 − 🐤 = ...

745  = ...

750 ⬭⬭ ⬭⬭ + 🐥🐥 = ...

PIGGY PENSHIP

HELP **PERCY** the pig TRACE the **WORDS**.

751 oink

752 mud

753 splash

754 pig

755 COLOR **PENELOPE** the **PIG**.

756

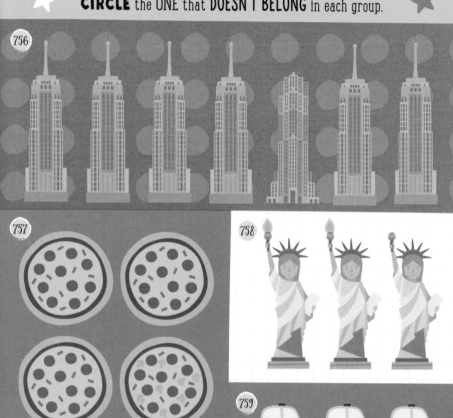

757

758

759

PIRATE PATTERNS

Add **COLOR** to FINISH the **PIRATE** patterns.

760

761

762

763

DEEP-SEA DIVERS

764 Finish **COLORING** the SCENE.

LOOK at the SCENE. ✔ the **BOXES** when you **FIND** the THINGS on the list.

767 6 fish

768 2 kronosaurus

769 1 octopus

770 4 shells

765 DRAW some **SPOTS** on the **KRONOSAURUS**.

766 DOODLE more JIGGLY **JELLYFISH** TENTACLES.

771 2 jellyfish

772 2 sea horses

773 3 underwater volcanoes

774 1 sea star

775

FIND and **CIRCLE** the FLAGS
that look **EXACTLY LIKE** these ones.

776

Use **COLOR** to **FINISH** the PATTERNS.

777

778

FARMYARD FINDS

SEARCH the **FARM** for the **THINGS** below.

✓ the boxes when you **FIND** them.

779
780
781
782

163

FUNNY FRAMES

COLOR the ANIMALS in the FRAMES.

786 **DRAW** funny HATS on the **PIGS**.

787 DRAW your **FAVORITE** ANIMAL in the frame.

WHAT is this animal **CALLED**? **WRITE** the MISSING LETTER.

788 g _ _ _

FEARSOME FRIENDS

789 DRAW DANNY some terrific **TEETH.**

790 COLOR the **VOLCANO.**

791 COLOR the **EGGS.**

792 FINISH the **FOOTPRINTS.**

793 ADD SPIKES to SAMMY the STEGOSAURUS' back.

794 GIVE TIMMY three **HORNS!**

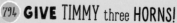

PIRATE QUIZ

WRITE the **LETTER** that **ANSWERS** each QUESTION below.

A

B

C

D

E

F

G

H

795 Who has an **EYE PATCH?**

....

796 Who has a **GRAY BEARD?**

....

797 Who has **BROWN BOOTS?**

....

167

SILLY SOUNDS

DRAW **LINES** to match each ANIMAL to its SOUND.

 BAA

 798

 799

NEIGH

OINK

 800

 801

MOO

 802

QUACK

JURASSIC JUMBLE

UNSCRAMBLE the WORDS below.
USE the PICTURES to **GUIDE** you.
Then **WRITE** the words on the DOTTED LINES.

DONISUAR

803 ....

RSKOC

804 ....

LASCW

805 ....

ESGG

806 ....

807 **HOW MANY**
BONES can you count?
WRITE the **ANSWER:** ....

169

TERRIFIC TRACE

HELP **CARLA** the cow TRACE the WORDS.

808 moo

809 cow

810 milk

811 fields

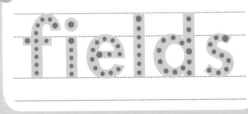

TRICKY TRAILS

FOLLOW the TRAILS to see which DINOSAUR gets the **CUPCAKES**.

812 Lil the Lambeosaurus

813 Tara the Tsintaosaurus

814 Sally the Stegosaurus

815 **DOODLE** some yummy **TOPPINGS** on the CUPCAKES.

OODLES OF EGGS

FIND and **CIRCLE** the EGGS that look like **THESE**.

816 817 818 819

820 **COPY** the EGG. Use the GRID to **HELP** you.

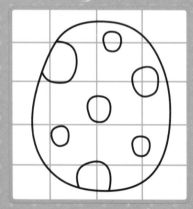

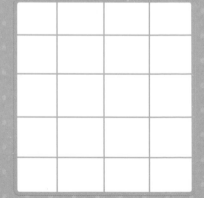

821 Then **COLOR** it in.

WOOLLY WANDER

GUIDE the **SHEEP** through the MAZE
to reach the MIDDLE of the **FIELD**.

822

Start

Finish

823
COLOR the KID.

824 **TRACE** the DOTS
to FINISH the FLOWERS.

PIRATE PUZZLER

This SCENE isn't QUITE RIGHT!
CIRCLE the SEVEN things that DON'T BELONG.

✔ the boxes when you **FIND** them.

825 [1] 826 [2] 827 [3] 828 [4] 829 [5] 830 [6] 831 [7]

WALK THE PLANK!

USE the **CLUES** to find out which PIRATE must WALK the PLANK.

First Mate Fi

Captain Clara

Sailor Shaun

Pirate Padma

Pirate Penny

Pirate Pablo

Sailor Susan

Captain Charlie

Captain Callum

Pirate Primrose

Captain Chris

Pirate Peter

CLUE 1:
The pirate has an eye patch.

CLUE 2:
The pirate has a gold earring.

CLUE 3:
The pirate has a hook.

832 WHO has to WALK the **PLANK?**

....
....

PIRATE TELESCOPES

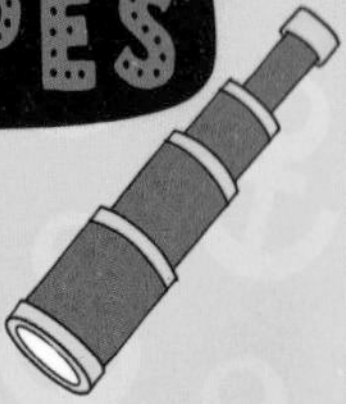

COLOR the IMAGES in the TELESCOPES.

833

834

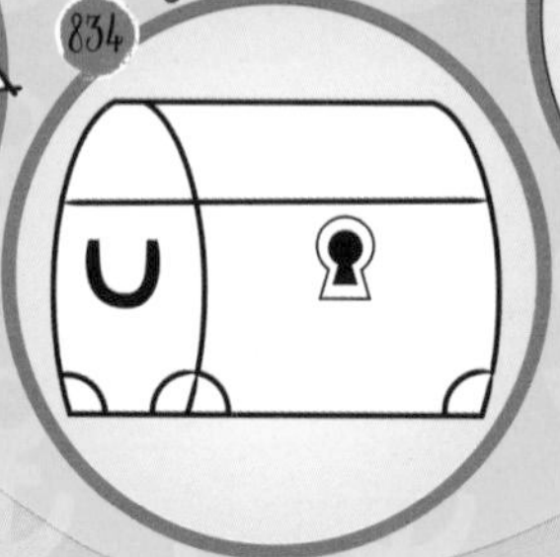

U

835

836 **COPY** the SHARK.
Use the GRID to HELP you.

837 Now **COLOR** it in.

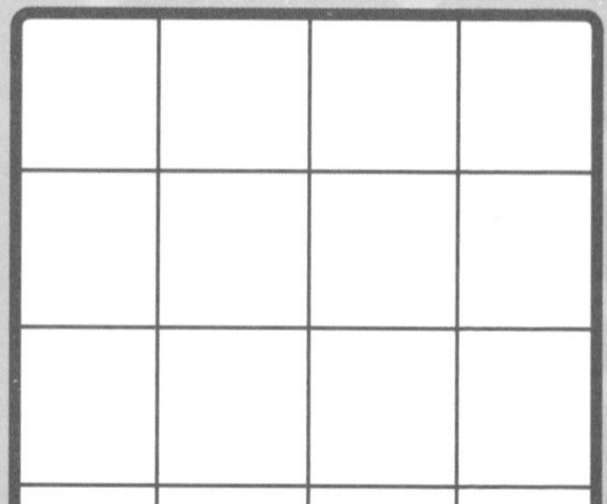

PERFECT PATTERNS

USE COLORS to **COMPLETE** the PATTERNS.

838

839

840

841

DEER TROUBLE

WRITE the LETTER that **ANSWERS** each QUESTION BELOW.

 A

 B

 C

 D

 E

 F

 G

 H

842 Who has **THREE SPOTS?**

....

843 Who has a **PINK NOSE?**

....

844 Who has **BLUE HOOVES?**

....

845 Who doesn't have **ANTLERS?**

....

178

FLYING HIGH

846 CONNECT the DOTS to REVEAL the PICTURE.

847 Then COLOR it in!

HOW MANY of the following ITEMS can you see on THIS PAGE?

848 dragonfly

849 bird

850 cloud

851 flower

PIRATE PAIRS

DRAW LINES between each **PIRATE**
and the **MATCHING** colored **JEWELS**.

852  purple

853  red

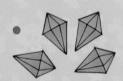

854  blue

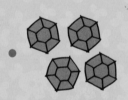

855  green

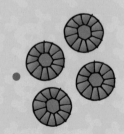

WINTER WISHES

Search the **GRID** for the **WINTER** words below.
WORDS can go DOWN or **ACROSS**.

 each WORD when you've **FOUND IT**.

i	g	l	o	o	x	z	e	i	l
x	r	p	q	s	c	a	r	f	u
q	v	e	t	d	o	u	s	q	m
w	f	n	h	x	a	e	f	x	i
s	e	g	n	v	t	b	j	u	t
h	i	u	l	s	q	z	k	e	t
j	m	i	c	e	x	w	s	c	e
i	w	n	q	j	h	a	t	d	n
e	x	v	z	h	s	d	r	e	s
s	n	o	w	m	a	n	q	t	x

856

coat

857

hat

858

ice

859

igloo

860

mittens

861

penguin

862

scarf

863

snowman

181

THE CROWN JEWELS

COMPLETE the **SUMS** to HELP the KING **COUNT** his jewels.

864

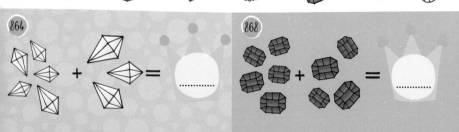 + = ...

868

+ = ...

865

+ = ...

869

+ = ...

866

+ = ...

870

+ = ...

867

+ = ...

871

+ = ...

182

PIRATE PORTRAITS

872 **DRAW** a **PIRATE** in the frame.

873 **DESIGN** a pirate **FLAG**.

874 **DOODLE** a **MUSTACHE** on **CAPTAIN STEVE**.

875 **COLOR** MOLLY MATE'S BANDANA.

183

PRETTY PONIES

876 **COLOR** the PONIES in the field.

877 **HOW MANY** HORSE SHOES can you count? WRITE the **ANSWER:** ....

878 **DECORATE** the SADDLE.

879 **COLOR** the RIDING HELMET.

WORD SCRAMBLER

UNSCRAMBLE the WORDS below.
USE the PICTURES to **GUIDE** you.
Then **WRITE** the words on the DOTTED LINES.

ESA

880 ....

NNNOAC

881 ....

RTUTEL

882 ....

GFAL

883 ....

884 **FIND** and CIRCLE all the **COINS** that look like **THIS:**

185

READY, STEADY, RACE!

885 **TRACE** the **DOTS** to finish TINA the PTERODACTYL'S **WINGS**.

886 Then **COLOR** them in!

887 **GUIDE** TOM the T.REX through the **MAZE** to **ESCAPE** the **VOLCANO**.

Finish

Start

HORSING AROUND

HELP **HENRY** the HORSE to TRACE the WORDS.

888 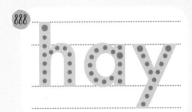 hay

889 farm

890 barn

891 horse

892 **COLOR** HATTY the HORSE.

SEASIDE SEARCH

FIND and **CIRCLE** the **FOUR** things that look like **THIS:**

893   *894*   *895*   *896*

✔ the **BOXES** when you **FIND** them.

188

FANCY FIREWORKS

The **DINOSAURS** are having a **CELEBRATION**.

897 **DRAW** an amazing FIREWORK display.

898 **CIRCLE** the DINO that is DIFFERENT.

SUPER SUMMER

FIND all EIGHT EMOTIS in the grid.
WORDS can go DOWN or **ACROSS**.

899 cactus

900 pineapple

901 octopus

902 sandals

x	q	s	s	a	n	d	a	l	s
p	a	u	w	z	e	q	x	z	o
i	j	n	x	w	h	a	l	e	v
n	u	g	o	q	z	c	o	f	i
e	q	l	c	a	c	t	u	s	a
a	h	a	t	d	l	z	q	u	c
p	m	s	o	t	m	p	u	n	q
p	x	s	p	q	v	s	c	x	w
l	w	e	u	x	s	h	e	l	l
e	g	s	s	t	x	t	v	s	k

903 sun

904 shell

905 sunglasses

906 whale

907 **COLOR** the **BEACH** scene.

190

SHIP SHAPE

LABEL the **PIRATE SHIP** using the WORDS listed below:

908 anchor   909 deck   910 plank
911 cannon   912 flag   913 porthole
914 crow's nest   915 mast   916 sail

c _ _ _ _ 's
n _ _ _ _

f _ a _

s _ _ l

c _ n _ _ _ _

p l _ _ k

d _ _ _ _

p _ _ t _ _ l _

m _ _ _ _

a _ c _ _ _ _

917 Now **COLOR** the PICTURE.

EMOTI ART

Use the **GRID** to FINISH the **EMOTIS** BELOW.

ROBOT

918

919 Now. **COLOR** the ROBOT.

PANDA

920
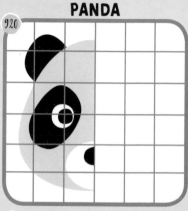

921 **ADD** some colorful LEAVES!

MOON

922

923 **DOODLE** some STARS behind it.

LION

924

925 Now. **COLOR** the LION.

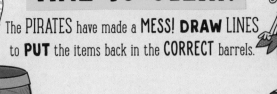

TIME TO CLEAN

The PIRATES have made a MESS! **DRAW** LINES
to **PUT** the items back in the **CORRECT** barrels.

926

927

928

929

DINO DOODLES

930 **COLOR** the **DINOSAURS**.

931 Now **GIVE** them funny **NAMES!**

932 **DRAW** your own **DINOSAUR** in the space below.

ALL ABOARD!

FIND and CIRCLE the SHIPS that look EXACTLY LIKE these ones.

935 COLOR the **SCENE**.

ALL AT SEA

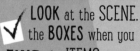

LOOK at the SCENE.
✓ the BOXES when you
FIND the ITEMS on the list.

936
4 pirates ☐

940
1 sea star ☐

937
1 crab ☐

941
4 portholes ☐

938
3 parrots ☐

942
1 treasure chest ☐

939
1 anchor ☐

943
3 shells ☐

944 DOODLE a DESIGN for the **PIRATE SAIL.**

945 COLOR the **SUN.**

TIME TO TRACE

HELP **LUCY** the lamb to **TRACE** the **WORDS**.

946 lamb

947 wool

948 sheep

949 spring

FIND THE ANSWER

CIRCLE the PICTURES to **ANSWER** the QUESTIONS.

950 **WHICH** one DOESN'T **SAIL?**

951 **WHICH** one DOESN'T **FLY?**

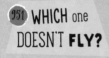

952 **WHICH** one DON'T you **WEAR?**

953 ADD **COLOR** to the page.

DREAM PETS

In the FRAMES, **DRAW** EMOTIS of your dream PETS.
GIVE your pets NAMES in the spaces below!

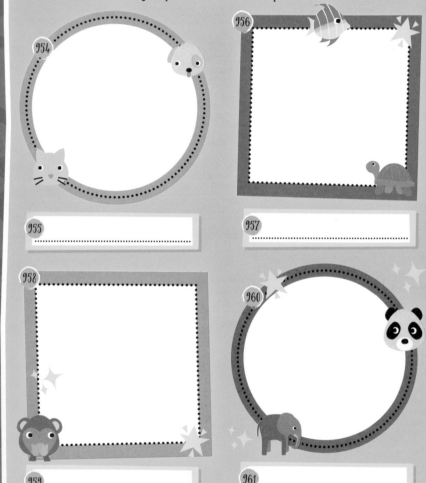

954

956

955

957

958

959

960

961

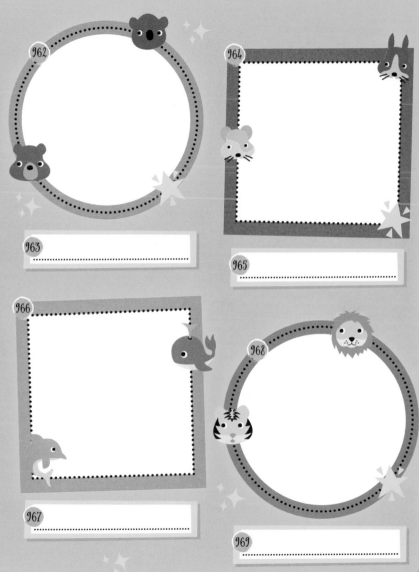

962

963

964

965

966

967

968

969

DINOSAUR DIG

970 HOW MANY FOOTPRINTS can you count? WRITE the **ANSWER:** ....

971 COLOR the FOSSIL.

a	x	p	l	a	n	t	c	k	o
t	s	v	n	m	d	a	a	j	u
s	k	i	x	w	n	i	f	u	s
i	u	m	u	t	t	l	e	r	v
c	l	o	f	i	j	o	z	a	z
u	l	b	o	n	e	l	x	s	k
x	v	t	s	q	w	q	r	s	e
q	d	x	s	x	i	a	o	i	q
w	p	w	i	c	l	x	u	c	t
u	o	h	l	r	o	c	k	s	x

FIND the **WORDS** in the WORD SEARCH. WORDS can go DOWN or **ACROSS**.

972 bone

973 fossil

974 jurassic

975 plant

976 rocks

977 skull

978 tail

TRACTOR TROUBLE

979 **GUIDE** the **TRACTOR** through the MAZE to reach the **MIDDLE** of the field.

980 **DRAW** a HAPPY FACE on the **SUN**.

Start

Finish

981 **COLOR** the ROOSTER.

COIN DROP

Follow the **LINES** to see which
PIRATE has dropped COINS overboard.

982

983

984

985 COLOR the **CANNON**.

SPORTS DAY

Add **COLOR** to finish the **SPORTY** PATTERNS.

986

987

988

989

DINO DISCO

Can you find SIX **DIFFERENCES** between the SCENES?

✓ the boxes when you **FIND** them.

990 | 1 | 991 | 2 | 992 | 3 | 993 | 4 | 994 | 5 | 995 | 6

EMOTI ESTIMATES

Look at the **EMOTIS** in each section. HOW MANY do you **THINK** there are?
WRITE your **ESTIMATES**, and then **COUNT** them to see if you were right!

996 robots — WRITE your ESTIMATE: ....

997 trophies — WRITE your ESTIMATE: ....

998 cheese burgers — WRITE your ESTIMATE: ....

999 dogs — WRITE your ESTIMATE: ....

TIME FOR BED

1,000

COLOR the SCENE.

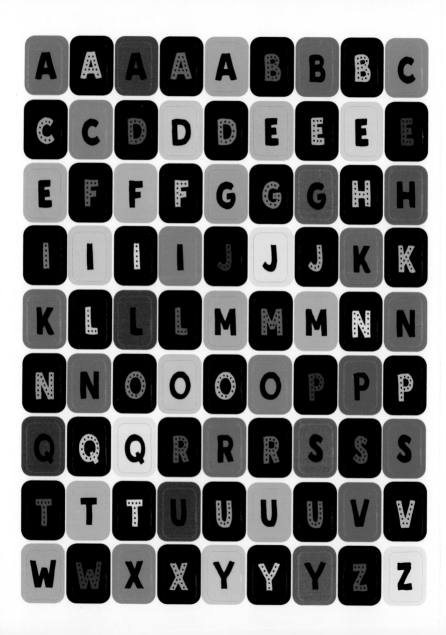